The Ugly Duckling

Retold by
Susanna Davidson

Illustrated by
Daniel Postgate

Reading Consultant: Alison Kelly
Roehampton University

"I have six eggs," said Mother Duck.

Five eggs were smooth
and small and white.

But the
sixth egg was
huge.

All spring, the mother
duck sat on her eggs,
waiting for them to hatch.
She waited...

and waited...

and waited...

5

Until at last...

Hooray!

...one of the eggs went **tap, tap, tap!**

"Hurry!" Mother Duck
called to the other ducks.
"Come and see!"

"My eggs are hatching!"

One egg shell after
another burst open.

"Come out! Come out!"
called Mother Duck...

...and the ducklings came
tumbling out.

They looked all around,
at the tall grasses and the
green leaves.

10

"Is everyone here?" asked
Mother Duck.

But the big egg still
hadn't hatched.

"Looks like a turkey egg to me," said an old duck. "I think you should leave it!"

"I'll just wait a little bit longer," said Mother Duck.

12

And at last, the great
egg burst open.

"Cheep! Cheep!" said the
duckling, looking out.

13

Mother Duck gasped.
The old duck spluttered.

The duckling was very
large and very ugly.

"It *is* a turkey chick," said the old duck. "Take it swimming. Then you'll see."

So Mother Duck took her ducklings down to the pond. One by one, they all jumped in.

17

The dark water closed
over their heads.

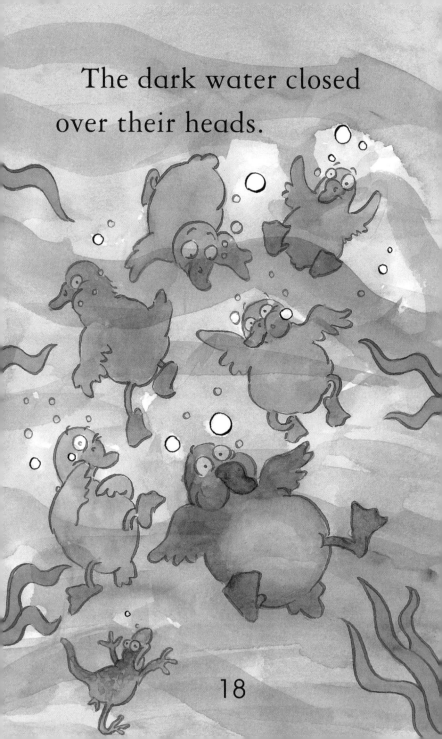

The next moment,
they all popped up again.

"You can swim! You're not a turkey chick," said Mother Duck.

"You're just a very
ugly duckling."

Mother Duck took her
ducklings to the farmyard.

The geese laughed at the
Ugly Duckling and the
hens pecked at it.

The turkey puffed himself up until he was red in the face. Then he gobbled at it.

The farmboy shooed the Ugly Duckling away.

Out of my way!

He flew over the fence...

...and into a bush.

"Nobody wants me,"
said the Ugly Duckling.
"I'm too ugly."

He ran on and on.

At last he came to
a great swamp, where
the wild ducks lived.

The Ugly Duckling hid in
the swamp all night long.

In the morning, the wild ducks looked at him and laughed. "You're so ugly," they said. But then...

BOOOOM!

BANG!

Gun shots flew through the air. The wild ducks took off in fright.

A great hunt was going on.

Hunting dogs splashed
through the swamp.

Splash!

The Ugly Duckling hid
his head under his wing.

At that moment a fierce
dog with glaring eyes,
came up to the duckling.

It stuck out its nose
and showed its sharp teeth.
But it didn't bite.

At last, late in the day,
the gun shots stopped.

The Ugly Duckling ran
out of the swamp as fast as
he could.

It was so windy, he got blown this way...

...and that.

As darkness fell, the Ugly
Duckling reached an old
house. He crept inside.

"Can I stay here?"
asked the Ugly Duckling.

"Can you lay eggs?"
asked a hen.

"No," said the Ugly
Duckling.

"Can you purr?" hissed
a cat.

"I don't think so," said
the Ugly Duckling.

"Then get out," said the
cat, swiping at the
duckling with its paw.

The duckling went away
to a large lake.

He swam and dived
every day.

But no animal would talk to
him because he was so ugly.

The weather grew colder.
The leaves turned yellow
and brown and danced in
the wind.

One evening, just as the
sun was setting, a flock of
birds flew across the sky.

The duckling had never
seen anything so beautiful.

The birds were shining
white with long, smooth
necks. They were swans.

The weather grew colder
and colder.

The Ugly Duckling
almost froze in the ice.

But when spring came,
the Ugly Duckling was still
alive. He lay in the reeds and
listened to the birds sing.

The Ugly Duckling raised
his wings. They beat the air
more strongly than before.

He flew and flew, until he came to a garden with a pond and three glorious swans.

The swans came closer,
flapping their wings.

"Perhaps they'll peck me
and bite me," thought the
Ugly Duckling.

He bent his head to the
water and saw...

...that he was no longer
an ugly duckling. He was
a swan!

The other swans swam
around him and stroked
him with their beaks.

Then a family of ducks
came into the garden. They
gazed at the swans.

"Look! A new one's
arrived," they said.

"And he's the most beautiful one of all!"

The Ugly Duckling was first told by Hans Christian Andersen, who was born in Denmark in 1805. When he was young he was shy and awkward, but he grew up to be famous all over the world for his wonderful fairy tales.

Series editor: Lesley Sims

Designed by
Russell Punter and Louise Flutter

First published in 2006 by Usborne Publishing Ltd., Usborne House, 83-85 Saffron Hill, London EC1N 8RT, England. www.usborne.com
Copyright © 2006 Usborne Publishing Ltd.

The right of Daniel Postgate to be identified as the Illustrator of this Work has been asserted by him in accordance with the Copyright Designs and Patents Act 1988.

48